Critterlandia

Whimsical stories and facts for animal lovers

Robin M. Strand and David J. Sacks

Illustrated by Robin M. Strand

To the precious animals of Earth and all who are fascinated by them

And

To Vincent, Seamus, and Minutia - three of the world's most wonderful cats

Acknowledgments

Special thanks are due to reviewers of a draft of this book. Because of their very helpful feedback and encouragement, this book is even better than it otherwise would have been:

Linda Evans

Kelly Morales

Margaret Strand

Kyra Termini

Susan Termini

Christy Walsh

Contents

A Few Words About the Stories

Animals are everywhere. And in great numbers. Scientists estimate that there are over seven million(!) different species of animals on Earth's lands and in Earth's waters. These animals live fascinating lives of their own with all sorts of experiences we often know little about. The authors came to writing Critterlandia by wondering: What if we could eavesdrop on animals' previously unknown thoughts and adventures?

So, Critterlandia tells short stories about animals, in the form of poems. The stories present animals as if they are like people in various ways. (The fancy word for that is anthropomorphism.) Just as people sometimes act in odd and unexpected ways, Critterlandia tells about the quirky activities of animals while remaining true to the animals' actual attributes.

A page titled "By the Way" follows each story. Each By the Way includes a few facts about the real-world animal that hopefully lead readers to think "I didn't know that - that's really interesting!" The By the Ways mention the formal names scientists have assigned to the animal or to a group to which the animal belongs. While these names are interesting, don't fret when you try to pronounce them because the truth is that hardly anyone other than scientists knows how to pronounce them.

Near the end of this book you can find a map showing the major locations mentioned in the stories, and where to find additional information on the animals.

Animals – from the smallest and simplest to the largest and most advanced – are each fascinating in their own way. The authors had a lot of fun writing about the animals and hope you have even more fun reading about them.

It's Time to Begin

Welcome – An Aye-Aye Hi

Hola
Spanish

Aloha
Hawaiian

こんにちは
Japanese

Y ou woke me up, you startled me

I wish you'd let me rest

Why are you up here in my tree?

This is my private nest

Hallo
German

Hello
English

You say you came to visit me

I grudgingly say "Hi"

But I'd prefer you leave me be

مرحبا
Arabic

And here's the reason why

שלום
Hebrew

I know I look adorable

So you may want to pet me

But that makes me uncomfortable

I'm shy – it would upset me

It's not true that I bring bad luck

Though that's what some folks say

Don't bother me, just leave me be

Or else I'll run away

By the Way. . .

The aye-aye is a small mammal with brownish fur and big brown eyes. It can grow to be about 3 feet (.9 meters) long, more than half of which is just its bushy tail. Aye-ayes live on the island of Madagascar which is located near the southeast coast of Africa. They live most of their lives in trees.

Aye-ayes have unusual fingers they use to help find food. One very long, thin finger is used to tap on logs and branches to find areas where insects live. The aye-aye then bites that area to expose insects underneath and uses an even longer finger to pull the insects out.

The aye-aye is a kind of mammal called a lemur. There are about 100 different animals that are lemurs, some of which have rather unusual names such as the hairy-eared dwarf lemur and Madame Berthe's mouse lemur. Lemurs are native to Madagascar and some small nearby islands. (Madagascar is the native home of many animals not found anywhere else on Earth.) The word *lemur* comes from a word in ancient Roman mythology that means ghosts or spirits.

Some folks believe aye-ayes bring bad luck. Some even believe an aye-aye can kill people just by pointing at them with its long middle finger. Of course, this is mere superstition – or perhaps that's what aye-ayes want us to think.

The aye-aye is a species of animal with the scientific name Daubentonia madagascariensis.

A video side trip: A close-up view of an aye-aye searching for and eating an insect larva in a tree can be found by searching https://www.youtube.com/ for *aye-aye demon primate.*

Albatross at a Loss

The albatross was at a loss

To find some company

But that's the strife

Of one whose life

Is always spent at sea

One day he tried to make some friends

With squids and shrimps and fishes

But they were wary

And found him scary

Though he found them delicious!

By the Way. . .

Albatrosses are large birds that range over parts of the world's oceans. Their nests are on islands. Albatrosses have large wingspans that can be up to 12 feet (3.7 meters) across. They eat fish, squid, and small shrimp-like animals called krill. Albatrosses can live as long as 50 years.

An albatross plays an important role in the poem *The Rime of the Ancient Mariner* by Samuel Taylor Coleridge. The mariner, as punishment for killing an albatross, had to wear the dead bird around his neck. Because that poem is widely known, a person who faces an obstacle or bears an emotional burden is sometimes said to have "an albatross around his neck."

There are many species of albatrosses. They have informal names such as the Indian yellow-nosed albatross, the shy albatross, and the wandering albatross. All the different species of albatrosses are in a group of animals that scientists call Diomedeidae. (That's a mouthful even for an Albatross!)

Amsterdam Hamster

Amsterdam in the Netherlands

Stays dry due to its dikes and dams

The smallest hole could start a flood

That turns the whole town into mud

Once when it rained day after day

Folks hoped their dams would not give way

But as the waters reached their peak

The weakest dam began to leak

Morrie the hamster was nearby

And fast as the blink of an eye

He put a paw into that dam

This hamster thus saved Amsterdam

By the Way. . .

About the story: Amsterdam is the capital city of the Kingdom of the Netherlands in Europe. The name "Amsterdam" reflects the city's origins near a dam in the river Amstel.

Hamsters are small mammals. They have short fur that is typically black, brown, gray, white, or a combination. While they are similar to mice in appearance, hamsters generally have much shorter tails.

Wild hamsters are found throughout Europe and Asia. The species that is most popular as a house pet originated in Syria and is known as the Syrian hamster or the golden hamster. Syrian hamsters of various colors have been given informal names including black bear, European black bear, honey bear, panda bear, polar bear, teddy bear, and Dalmatian. (That prompts some important questions: Why all these bears and only one dog? And, in any case, why do some hamsters and bears have the same name?)

In the wild, hamsters feed mainly on fruits, seeds, and vegetation. They will even occasionally even eat burrowing insects. (It's not clear whether hamsters consider eating insects a treat – or an act of desperation.) They have large cheek pouches in which they can carry food back to their burrows. When full, their cheeks can make their heads double or larger in size (which means that telling a hamster it has a swelled head, rather than being a criticism, simply acknowledges it is a good forager).

Hamsters are popular house pets. Owners typically keep a pet hamster in a cage equipped with a hamster wheel that allows the hamster to run as exercise without actually going anywhere. (It's uncertain whether the hamster knows it's not going anywhere. It presumably enjoys the activity in any case.) Some owners provide their hamsters with hamster balls, small hollow balls with air holes in which a hamster is placed, allowing it to exercise by rolling the ball around from the inside.

There are about 25 different species of hamsters.   All species of hamsters – as well as related animals such as gerbils, mice, porcupines, and squirrels – belong to a group of animals that scientists call Rodentia (which, not surprisingly, is related to the term *rodent*).

Annoyed Zooid

("zooid" is pronounced: zoh'-oid.)

I'm just a simple zooid

Who wants to be alone

But I live in a colony

And can't be on my own

I'm just one zooid in a group

There're others left and right

They poke and prod me all the time

Which makes me feel uptight

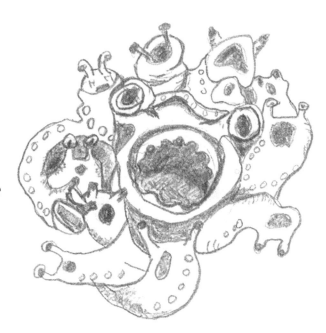

In the group that I am in

My role is clear to me

But I'd be happy on my own

To drift upon the sea

By the Way. . .

A zooid is actually not an animal. It is a tiny organism called a cell that lives in the water. Multiple zooids are attached together to form a colony that is an animal with its own name. Each zooid in a colony has a specific function it performs such as feeding or defending against predators.

Coral is a type of zooid colony. Another type of zooid colony is the Portuguese man o' war that lives at the surface of oceans, mostly in the tropics; it has tentacles that dangle below the water surface and can deliver a painful sting to swimmers. Some zooid colonies are long, thin, transparent animals that float on the water. Some of those colonies are up to about 160 feet (49 meters) in length which is the longest known animal.

Human beings, at first glance, might seem similar to zooids. After all, our bodies consist of individual cells with specialized functions and each human being as a whole is an independent animal. So, how are human beings different than zooids? A few major differences are that we have different physical forms than zooid, we live on land, and we have highly developed brains that provide our ability to read and write about zooids, rather than zooids reading and writing about us.

Animals made of zooids are in a group of animals that scientists call Siphonophorae.

Ant That Can't

"Stop your snoring!" Lion told Ant.

"I never snore! I'm small, I can't!

"I'll prove it - I'll go back to sleep.

You'll see, you will not hear a peep."

So Ant went back to sleep once more

And snored as loud as Lion's roar

15

By the Way. . .

Ants are small insects, typically black, brown, or red in color. Ants range in size from about .03 inches to 2 inches (0.8 to 52 millimeters). They live in colonies and large colonies may contain millions of individual ants. Different ants in a colony have different roles such as workers and queens; only queens can lay eggs.

Ants are found on each of the Earth's continents except Antarctica. (One way to help remember that fact, just in case that's something you want to do, is noticing that the word *ant* just happens to be the first part of the word *Antarctica*.)

Ants have a reputation for being hard workers. Some ants can lift an object far over 100 times their own weight! Aesop's fable, *The Ant and the Grasshopper*, tells the story of an industrious ant that works hard to save food for the harsh winter, while a lazy grasshopper ends up going hungry.

Scientists estimate there are over 20,000 separate species of ants. Some of these species have strange informal names like fire ant and yellow crazy ant. A list of all the scientific names of ant species would require another book and would probably bore you, so we'll just mention that all species of ants are in a group of animals that scientists call Formicidae. (Some ants can defend themselves by secreting *formic* acid when they bite their enemies.)

<u>A video side trip</u>: The activities of a very interesting type of ant called a leafcutter ant can be seen by searching https://www.youtube.com for w*here are the ants carrying all those leaves*.

Beak Mystique

I have a problem keeping neat

To preen I have to use my feet

The cause is my unique physique

My body's shorter than my beak!

By the Way. . .

Most birds use their beaks to groom and care for their feathers, a process called preening. In contrast, the beak of the sword-billed hummingbird – which this story is about – is so long that it isn't used for preening. Instead, this bird uses its feet for preening.

The sword-billed hummingbird lives in several different countries in South America. It has the remarkable attribute that its long beak, about 4 inches (10 centimeters) in length, is actually longer than its body not counting its tail. When perched, this bird must sit with its long beak pointing up to avoid toppling over.

Hummingbirds are among the Earth's smallest birds. They can flap their wings very rapidly, creating a humming sound. Unlike other birds, hummingbirds can hover in place, allowing them to remain nearly stationary in the air as they feed by inserting their thin beaks – also called *bills* – into flowers to extract the sugary nectar inside, or into birdfeeders containing sugar water. Hummingbirds also eat some kinds of insects.

The scientific species name of the sword-billed hummingbird is Ensifera ensifera.

A video side trip: A sword-billed hummingbird using its feet to preen can be seen by searching http://www.arkive.org within the "videos" category for *sword-billed hummingbird preening*.

Bear Cub Belly Rub

A hungry bear cub, cute and small

Found a honeypot, ate it all

Soon she got a bellyache

"Please fix it, Mommy, for goodness sake!"

So Mommy rubbed her tender tummy

And warned, "Next time, less honey, honey!"

By the Way. . .

Bears are medium to large mammals found in North America, South America, Asia, and Europe. Bears are good runners, climbers, and even swimmers. They use shelters, such as caves and burrows, as their dens. Most bears live in these dens during the winter for up to 100 days in a sleep-like state called *hibernation*.

While it is true that bears love to eat honey, they eat plants and animals as well – sometimes even the bees in a hive!

There are several species of bears living today, including those commonly known as brown bears, grizzly bears, panda bears, polar bears, and teddy bears. Well, not really teddy bears. A teddy bear is a soft toy named after U.S. President Theodore "Teddy" Roosevelt. "Teddy Bears Picnic," a song written in the early nineteen hundreds, has been recorded by many artists.

There are eight living species of bears. The scientific name for the group of animals that includes all species of bears is Ursidae. *Ursus* is the Latin word for bear. A famous constellation of stars in the northern night sky is Ursa Major, meaning great bear. Ursa Major is also known as the Big Dipper because it is shaped like a ladle. A nearby constellation is Ursa Minor, meaning smaller bear and also known as the Little Dipper.

Camping Koala

A camping koala

From an Australian town

Went camping "down under"

And slept under down

By the Way. . .

The koala is a small mammal that mainly eats eucalyptus leaves. It is native to Australia, a continent often called "the land down under" due to its location south of the equator.

The koala has a small body, no tail, fluffy ears, and a very noticeable, blackish nose. The koala's body is up to about 33 inches (85 centimeters) long. Some koalas have brownish fur while others have grayish fur.

Koalas are relatively inactive animals that sleep up to 20 hours a day. Because of their cute, teddy bear-like appearance, koalas are popular with zoo visitors and as stuffed toy animals.

Koalas appear in the myths of native Australians. In one myth, the reason koalas have no tails is because another Australian animal to which Koalas are related, the kangaroo, cut their tails off to punish koalas for being lazy.

The scientific species name of the koala is Phascolarctos cinereus.

Caterpillar Contribution

lastic?

Fantastic!

Pollution!

Solution?

Waxworm contribution!

By the Way. . .

<u>About the story</u>: Plastic bags are a *fantastic* invention because they are stronger than paper bags and can be transparent. However, plastic bags add to *pollution* because they are made of a material that doesn't easily break down so that it can be reused. The *solution* is to take advantage of a special capability of a caterpillar called the *waxworm*.

A waxworm is the caterpillar of a type of moth called a wax moth. The caterpillar's body is yellowish in color and has a worm-like appearance. Waxworms are found all over the world. They are often found in bee colonies where they eat the beeswax used to build honeycombs, which explains how the caterpillar got its name.

Waxworms are of special interest to scientists because waxworms have the ability to eat and digest a type of plastic called polyethylene. This type of plastic is used to make plastic bags. Unfortunately, these plastic bags pollute the environment because, unlike paper bags, they can take decades to break down into chemicals normally found in nature.

Because many people use plastic bags only once and then throw them out, a huge number of bags pile up in garbage dumps. (And, as you may have noticed, discarded bags also tend to be blown around by the wind, often ending up stuck in tree branches.) Scientists hope to identify the substance waxworms use to break down polyethylene plastic, so the substance could be reproduced in large amounts. It could then be used in recycling plants or sprayed on garbage dumps to reduce the time it takes plastic bags to break down.

There are three species of wax moths. One species of wax moth that has been observed to eat and digest polyethylene plastic is the greater wax moth which has the scientific species name Galleria mellonella.

Clam I am

I'll tell you the story of how I found glory

And why I am named Ming the Clam

A calm life I had led

In my comfy sea bed

'Til I found myself in a jam

In 2006 in the ocean near Iceland

One day in a net I was caught

So rudely disturbed

And pretty perturbed

"Now what do I do?" was my thought

"You really should know," I explained to my captors

"I'm too old for chowder or stew.

So, rather than bake me

Let scientists date me.

You'll see what I say is quite true.

"Don't take it on faith but when Henry the Eighth

Was alive, I was living as well.

So I'd be elated

To be carbon-dated

Or please count the bands on my shell."

The testing results showed my claim to be truthful

No one is as old as I am

I was born in the sea

In the Ming dynasty

So now I am called Ming the clam

To eat me at my age would be such an outrage

I deserve a much better fate

If I may be so bold

At 500 years old

I should be renamed Ming the Great!

By the Way. . .

Clams have two roundish shells connected by a hinge-like structure at one end. Mussels, oysters, and scallops also have hinged shells and are related to clams.

One day in 2006, a clam, later named Ming, was harvested off the coast of Iceland. Scientists determined it was about 507 years old based on the number of growth bands in its shell and also by a scientific technique called carbon dating. The test results indicated Ming was born in 1499, only a few years after King Henry VIII of England was born in 1491 and even fewer years after Columbus sailed to the Americas in 1492. That makes Ming the oldest individual animal known to have lived – ever!

The expression "happy as a clam" is a shortened version of "happy as a clam at high water." Because clams live partially buried in the ocean floor, that phrase may refer to clams being relatively safe from predators digging them up during high tide at which time they are difficult to find.

Ming belonged to a species of clam with the scientific name Arctica islandica. That species is informally known as the black clam, black quahog, mahogany clam, mahogany quahog, or ocean quahog.

Crab Crib

A small hermit crab
Found a small, empty shell
Claimed that shell for its home
Since it fit the crab well

The crab ate so much
It outgrew that small shell
Which now was quite cramped
And no longer fit well

So it wriggled out
Of that old smallish shell
And started to search
For a new place to dwell

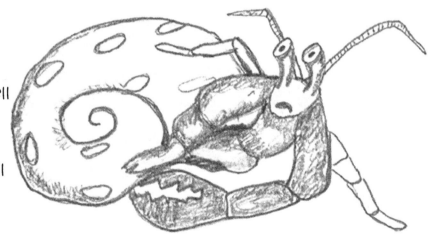

"But what if I can't
Find a large enough space?
I need something big
Yet not commonplace."

(In crab real estate

Certain things remain true

The size must be right

With a fine ocean view)

"My growing girth needs

A home that's gigantic.

Perhaps I should search for

The sunken Titanic!"

By the Way. . .

About the story: The Titanic was a huge British ocean liner that sank in the Atlantic Ocean in 1912 after colliding with an iceberg during her maiden voyage from England to the United States. The wreck of the ship is still at the bottom of the sea. The name "Titanic" is based on "Titans," gigantic gods in Greek mythology.

Hermit crabs live in the sea. They have soft bodies unprotected by a shell. They cleverly live in empty shells formerly inhabited by other sea creatures. The name "hermit crab" refers to the fact that these crabs each live alone like a human hermit, but in this case each crab lives in an empty shell it moves into and carries around with it. As hermit crabs grow, they abandon their shells and move into larger empty shells.

There are over 1000 species of hermit crabs. All these species are in a group of animals that scientists call crustacea. In addition to crabs, this group of animals also includes barnacles, crayfish, lobsters, and shrimp. Not surprisingly, members of this group are known as crustaceans.

A video side trip: To see a fascinating video showing hermit crabs cooperating to swap smaller shells for larger ones, search https://www.youtube.com for *amazing crabs shell exchange*.

Crocodile Smile

In a charming café on the bank of the Nile

With menu in hand sat a huge crocodile

The special that day

Was big beast sauté

So he ordered it raw with a smile!

By the Way. . .

Crocodiles are large reptiles, often grayish-green in color, that live in tropical climates. They spend time on land as well as in the water. Crocodiles have many sharp teeth that are visible even when their mouths are closed. Oddly, unlike other animals, crocodiles cannot stick out their tongues. Crocodiles feed mainly on other animals such as fish, birds, mammals, and even other reptiles.

A person may be said to be shedding "crocodile tears" if they are believed to be pretending to be sad. The term stems from an ancient belief that crocodiles weep when eating their victims. However, while crocodiles can generate tears, they do not actually cry based on their feelings the way humans do.

The most famous crocodile may be in the story *Peter Pan* by J. M. Barrie. The crocodile had eaten one of Captain Hook's arms after it was cut off by Peter Pan – the arm was replaced by a hook giving the pirate his name. That same crocodile also swallowed a clock that Captain Hook could hear ticking whenever the crocodile came near, typically resulting in Hook trembling with fear.

Crocodiles and alligators look very similar and people often find it difficult to tell them apart. One difference is in the shape of their snouts. Crocodiles have narrower and longer snouts than alligators, while alligators have more rounded snouts. There are other visible differences, but it is not recommended that the reader take a trip to the tropics to make a close inspection.

There are fourteen living species of crocodiles. These species have informal names such as the American crocodile, the Nile crocodile, the Philippine crocodile, and the Dwarf crocodile which is the smallest species of crocodile. All crocodile species, along with related animals such as alligators and caimans, belong to a group of animals that scientists call Crocodilia.

Cuttlefish Cuddle

Cuttlefish cuddle

At the sea's bottom

They hide so well that

It's hard to spot 'em

They can change texture

And also their hue

It looks just like magic

Performed right on cue

They can look checkered

Or spikey and spotted

Or look rainbow-colored

Or look polka-dotted

One cuttlefish said

To his mate (and I swear it!)

"I like you in red

So, please, would you wear it?"

"Of course!" she replied,

Turning red with delight

As they swam off happily

Into the night

By the Way. . .

Cuttlefish, in spite of their name, are actually not a type of fish, but a type of creature called a mollusk. Unlike fish, mollusks have soft bodies without a backbone. Cuttlefish inhabit warm waters along the coasts of Africa, Australia, East and South Asia, and Western Europe. They aren't found along the coasts of the Americas.

Cuttlefish are sometimes called the "chameleons of the sea" because of their amazing ability to quickly change the color, pattern, and even the texture of their skin. This helps them communicate with other cuttlefish as well as to hide from and scare off predators.

Cuttlefish mainly eat crabs and fish. Cuttlefish will sometimes eat other cuttlefish. That prompts an important question: If one cuttlefish looks at another cuttlefish in an affectionate way, is it being friendly or is it merely hungry?

Cuttlefish have an internal body structure called a cuttlebone. People often place cuttlebones in the cages of birds, such as parakeets, to provide a source of dietary calcium.

There are many species of cuttlefish. Cuttlefish are related to octopuses and squids because all these animals can eject dark ink to evade predators and all have multiple arms with suckers to help catch prey.

A video side trip: To see videos of cuttlefish actually changing their colors, search https://www.youtube.com for *cuttlefish colors*.

Draculouse

Beware the vile blood-sucking louse

If it should come into your house

Upon your scalp its jaws will munch

Your blood becomes its tasty lunch

It cares not if you're poor or rich

You'll start to twitch; you'll start to itch

You'll ask yourself: What should you do?

How ever do you make it shoo?

Politely ask it just to go?

Or ship it off to Borneo?

Stand on your head or wear a hat?

Or hit it with a baseball bat?

Douse your head with maple syrup?

Promise it a trip to Europe?

Chase it with a fine-toothed comb?

Threaten to burn down its home?

The louse will laugh; the louse will smirk

'Cause those ideas never work

No reason to endure the pain

Shampoo that louse right down the drain

By the Way. . .

<u>About the story</u>: *Dracula* is a novel written by Irish author Bram Stoker in 1897. The main character, Count Dracula, is a vampire: a being that survives by feeding on human blood.

A louse (plural: lice) is a type of small, wingless insect. Lice are found all over the world. They are parasites of birds and mammals, meaning they live off of those animals. Some types of lice eat an animal's skin while other types suck an animal's blood. Blood-sucking lice range in length from about .02 inches (.5 millimeters) to .20 inches (5 millimeters).

While a person infested with the type of lice that live in human hair may suffer from an itchy scalp, the good news is that head lice do not carry disease. Special combs and shampoos can be used to get rid of this pest.

In 1786, the Scottish poet Robert Burns wrote *To A Louse: On Seeing One On A Lady's Bonnet, At Church*. Burns was not shy about expressing his feelings about lice. Here are two lines from his poem:

> Ye ugly, creepin, blastit wonner,
> Detested, shunn'd by saunt an' sinner

(In more modern English: You ugly, creeping, blasted wonder / Detested, shunned by saint and sinner.)

There are nearly 5,000 different species of lice.

Eau de Hippopotamus

Hippos open their mouths so wide

You'll be tempted to peek inside

But should you dare to get that near

There is something you should fear

Should you ever get too close

You will want to hold your nose

The stench will absolutely stink

It reeks far worse than you would think

The smell of rotten eggs so bad

Will very quickly drive you mad

Your head will spin, you'll faint away

A hippo's breath is no bouquet

By the Way. . .

The hippopotamus, or *hippo* for short, is a large, barrel-shaped, grayish mammal that lives in Africa. The only land mammals that are larger are the elephant and rhinoceros. The name hippopotamus comes from a Greek term meaning "river horse" – hippos spend a lot of time in the water to keep cool. Perhaps that's not surprising considering that hippos are related to whales and porpoises.

A hippo's mouth contains numerous teeth including two large tusk-like teeth. Its lips are about two feet wide. The hinge connecting its upper and lower jaw is far back in its mouth, allowing a hippo to open its mouth vertically almost 180 degrees.

Human culture has been influenced by hippopotamuses. For example, the Disney animated film *Fantasia* includes a segment with a hippopotamus in a tutu dancing to the ballet *Dance of the Hours*. (Dancing gracefully is likely not easy for anyone weighing about 3000 pounds (1361 kilograms) as hippos do.) Another example of how hippos have influenced culture is the novelty song "I Want a Hippopotamus for Christmas" that rose to number 24 on *Billboard* magazine's pop chart in December 1953. (Warning: A hippo may not be the best thing to request for Christmas in case you were to actually receive one.)

The scientific species name of the common hippopotamus is Hippopotamus amphibious. ("Amphibious" means suited for both land and water.)

A video side trip: A man once ended up in the mouth of a hippopotamus, yet survived and was able to describe the odor. You can read about it by searching https://www.youtube.com for *man swallowed by hippo lives*.

Another video side trip: It's not unusual for animals of different species to form friendships. In the early 2000s, a hippopotamus named Owen and a tortoise named Mzee became friends in a nature park in Kenya. To see a video about this remarkable friendship, search https://www.youtube.com for *owen mzee*.

Eggdentity Crisis

There once was an egg

A mother had laid

That opened with quite a loud crack!

The newborn then asked

"What am I?" and gasped

"Oh drat! I'm a chick, send me back!

"I'll look good to eat

My future looks bleak,"

The little chick wistfully sighed

"I fear it's my fate

To end up on a plate

Deliciously battered and fried.

"I'm feeling so blue

Oh, what can I do?

Perhaps I could go incognito.

In a parrot disguise

I'll avoid my demise

And not end up in a burrito!"

By the Way. . .

The chicken is a medium-sized domesticated bird that originated in Asia but has spread across the globe. In 2011 the United Nations estimated there are about 19 billion (19,000,000,000) chickens on earth. That's more than three chickens for every person! Many people use chickens as a source of meat, eggs, or both.

Various terms are used to describe different types of chickens. Female chickens are called hens, though before they are one year old, which is when they usually are able to lay their first eggs, they are called pullets. Male chickens are commonly called roosters or cocks. Baby chickens are called chicks.

It has become a tradition since ancient Roman times to save the wishbone, a small bone of a cooked chicken (or turkey) located near the breast bone. Two people each hold the different ends of a dried wishbone, each makes a wish, then they pull – whoever gets the longest piece supposedly gets their wish granted. If the pieces are the same size, both people get their wishes granted. (The chicken, if it could wish, would probably wish it hadn't been cooked in the first place.)

A famous question is: Which came first, the chicken or the egg? One point-of-view is that two non-chickens (or, perhaps, two almost-chickens) made the first egg that hatched the first true chicken.

A famous folktale about a chicken is called *Chicken Little* or *Henny Penny*. After an acorn falls on its head, Chicken Little runs around in fear telling other animals "The sky is falling." Over time, different versions of the story were created. In one version, the teaching is: Have courage rather than be a scared "chicken." In another version, a fox invites the animals to its lair for safety, following which it eats them all; the teaching is: Don't believe everything you hear.

The scientific name of the species of the domesticated chicken is Gallus gallus domesticus. (Yes, "gallus" really is repeated.) There are hundreds of breeds of domesticated chickens that vary in characteristics such as color or the country they live in. An example is the Australorp, an Australian breed of chicken with black feathers.

ENIAC Yak

In olden days before PC and MAC

A computer geek, a yak named Jack,

Searched high and low for a computer to hack

But all Jack could hack was an old ENIAC

By the Way. . .

About the story: ENIAC stands for *Electronic Numerical Integrator and Computer*. It was one of the earliest electronic computers and was used during the 1940s for military purposes. ENIAC was much larger, much more expensive, and much slower than today's personal computers.

Yaks are large, cattle-like mammals. Males may weigh up to about 2200 pounds (1000 kilograms). Both male and female yaks have horns. Yaks have long, dense, mostly brownish fur (also called wool) that hangs down and may even touch the ground. Their wool helps protect yaks against the cold.

There are two types of yaks: domestic yaks and wild yaks. The story is about the domestic yak, found throughout the Himalaya mountains of Asia and as far north as Mongolia and Russia. The domestic yak is descended from the wild yak.

Domestic yaks have been kept for thousands of years. They are valued for their milk, their meat, and for their wool used to make clothing, blankets, and more. (One of the authors (David) once was given Yak milk to drink – he didn't like it one bit.) Yaks are sometimes used by farmers and traders to transport goods across mountain passes, and are also used for climbing and trekking expeditions. Yaks are sometimes even ridden for racing.

The scientific species name of the domestic yak is Bos grunniens ("grunting ox"). The scientific species name of the wild yak is Bos mutus ("mute ox" – perhaps because it had nothing to say about the matter).

Fly on the Wall

Want to know what your friends say

When you're not there, but far away?

Oh, to be a fly on the wall

An eavesdropper, ever so small

You won't be seen while they are talking

You can spy on all their squawking

You'll soon know what they think of you

You'll hear it all; they'll have no clue

But, if by chance you they should spy

And have a swatter, it's goodbye fly!

By the Way. . .

<u>About the story</u>: The expression "a fly on the wall" means listening to a conversation or watching an event without being noticed. This type of expression is called an idiom because its meaning isn't obvious from the phrase.

The world is full of insects called flies: fruit flies, horseflies, houseflies, and other types of flies. Houseflies, found all over the world, make up the vast majority of flies found in homes. Many people think that houseflies are nothing but useless pests carrying germs around, a thought reflected in a clever poem by the 20th century American poet Ogden Nash:

> God in His wisdom made the fly
>
> And then forgot to tell us why

Nevertheless, the story is not all bad because flies help recycle waste in nature.

The common housefly's scientific species name is Musca domestica.

<u>A video side trip</u>:   A fly appears in the often-recorded children's song *There Was an Old Lady Who Swallowed a Fly*. This song tells the tale of a woman who swallowed a fly, then swallows animals of increasing sizes in attempts to catch the animal previously swallowed. A classic version of this song, sung by American singer and actor Burl Ives, can be heard by searching https://www.youtube.com for *burl ives I know an old lady*.

Gecko Cogitation

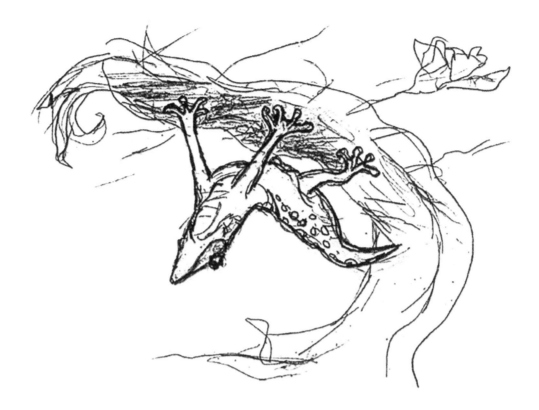

The gecko loves a good debate

He can make his case with feeling

From a point of view unique

Upside down upon the ceiling

By the Way. . .

Geckos are small reptiles known as lizards that live in warm climates around the world. A gecko's toes have the fascinating property of being able to cling to surfaces, allowing geckos to walk up walls and even walk across ceilings.

Geckos come in different colors and some can even change colors like a chameleon. Nearly all geckos do not have eyelids and, therefore, cannot blink; they lick their eyes to keep them moist and clean.

Geckos like to eat crickets, grasshoppers, and other small animals. If caught by their tails by predators, most geckos can escape by leaving their tails behind; some geckos can even regrow a tail lost this way.

There are over 1,650 different species of geckos worldwide. The informal names of some of these species include the bent-toed gecko, the crocodile gecko, the gold dust day gecko, and the western banded gecko.

Goat in a Boat with a Stoat

A goat stood by a riverbank

Munching a bunch of greenery

He felt ignored as well as bored

And wanted a change of scenery

A friend of the goat, a weasel-like stoat,

Happened to come along

She noticed her chum was looking quite glum,

So the stoat asked sincerely, "What's wrong?"

The goat replied, "I'm stressed, I'm depressed!

Whatever shall I do?"

"Come along with me!" said the stoat cheerily,

Let's have an adventure for two!"

"I've got a new boat" said the stoat to the goat,

And you can be my first mate!

With the breeze at our backs I'm sure you'll relax,

And soon you'll be feeling first rate!"

By the Way. . .

About goats

Goats are medium-size mammals found all over the world. Like cows and sheep, goats are ruminants. Ruminants have four-chambered stomachs. After a ruminant has partially digested its food, which is then called cud, ruminants regurgitate and rechew it (ugh!) as the next stage of digestion.

Goats have long played roles in mythology. The chariot of Thor, the god of Thunder in Norse mythology, is pulled by goats. Some mythological creatures are part goat and part human, such as the Greek god Pan who invented the pan flute (mythologically speaking, that is).

There are several species of goats, all of which are in a group of animals that scientists call Capra. (The astrological sign *Capricorn* has a goat's head and a fish's tail.) Some informal names for species of goats are wild goat and ibex. ("Ibex" can be a useful word to know for games like Scrabble and Words with Friends.)

About stoats

The stoat is a small mammal found throughout Asia, Europe, and North America. The stoat is also known as the short-tailed weasel.

Stoats mainly eat small rodents, though they will occasionally also eat fish, small birds, and even lizards and insects.

A stoat is sometimes called an ermine when it has white winter fur. Ermine fur has long been considered a luxury, although fake fur is sometimes substituted for it out of concern for animal rights.

The stoat's scientific species name is Mustela erminea.

Gone Fawn

A sleepy fawn

Woke up at dawn

Gave a big yawn

Then she was gone

By the Way. . .

A fawn is a young deer during its first year of life. Deer are mammals that are generally reddish, brownish, or grayish in color. Deer are native to all continents except Antarctica and Australia. Different species of deer vary in size.

> The smallest deer
>
> Is called a pudu
>
> Not two feet tall!
>
> Who knew? Now you do!

A female deer is known as a doe and a male deer is sometimes known as a stag. "Stag" also has another meaning based on the observation that at least some male deer species generally travel alone. In U.S. culture, a boy or man who attends a social gathering by himself is said to be "going stag." A gathering of only males is sometimes called "a stag party."

Many, though not all, deer have antlers. Antlers are a pair of bony structures that grow out of a deer's skull in a branching pattern. They help distinguish males from females. Deer with antlers typically shed their old antlers and grow new ones periodically. Horns, unlike antlers and found on animals such as rams and rhinoceroses, are permanent.

There are multiple species of deer. Deer, a term that is both singular and plural like "fish," belong to a group of animals that scientists have named Cervidae. Examples of the informal names of species of deer in this group include Chinese water deer, elk, moose, and reindeer (also known as caribou in North America).

Kitty Go Lightly

Minutia is a graceful cat

Kitten size, no ounce of fat

She moves quite lightly on her paws

In spite of having eighteen claws

Minutia doesn't like to fight

She'd rather dance away the night

She'd do a tap dance on a box

She'd even foxtrot with a fox

If she hears a concertina

She'll dance like a ballerina

Or if confronted by a mouse

She'll ask to dance a waltz by Strauss

Minutia loves to leap quite high

She seems to touch the bright blue sky

She smoothly hops and glides through space

Each move displays her feline grace

By the Way. . .

About the story: The title "Kitty Go Lightly" refers to a woman named Holly Golightly, a character in the book *Breakfast at Tiffany's* by Truman Capote. The book was later made into a popular movie.

Cats are small mammals found all over the world. Cats kept as house pets are often called *domestic cats* or *house cats*. Many people are surprised to learn that cats have eighteen claws, five on each front paw and four on each rear paw.

Cats have long played significant roles in human societies. Bastet, a goddess in ancient Egypt, had the head of a cat. A famous, more modern cat is the Cheshire Cat in *Alice's Adventures in Wonderland* by Lewis Carroll. Cats have a variety of personalities and seem to like showing off on the Internet.

The musical *Cats* has been performed in many countries. It is based on *Old Possum's Book of Practical Cats* by T. S. Eliot. *Cats* is a story about the night a tribe of cats decide which cat will ascend to heaven and come back to a new life. (You may have heard the myth that cats have nine lives.)

The domestic cat belongs to a group of animals that scientists call Felidae. (A common term for cats is "feline.") In addition to domestic cats, the Felidae group includes jaguars, leopards, lions, and tigers. The domestic cat's scientific species name is Felis catus. There are dozens of breeds of domestic cats that differ in size, color, length of fur, and temperament (such as more active or more quiet). Examples of breeds of domestic cats are Abyssinian, American Shorthair, Bengal, Burmese, Persian, Scottish Fold, and Siamese.

A video side trip: Cat lovers may enjoy videos of Henri the cat. Henri "thinks" out loud (in French with English subtitles) about his life with clever, dry humor. To see the videos, search https://www.youtube.com for *henrilechatnoir* (which is French for "Henri the black cat").

Long Live the Jellyfish

A special type of jellyfish

Starts young, grows old, then young again

If you were granted just one wish

Would it be to be that jellyfish?

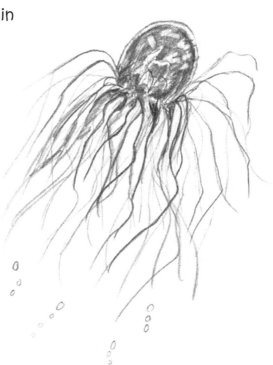

Your life would change for evermore

You'd swim the ocean end to end

With nothing new left to explore

Would life be fun, or just a bore?

By the Way. . .

A type of jellyfish known as the immortal jellyfish lives in the ocean. This jellyfish is very small at only up to .18 inches (4.5 millimeters) around and tall.

The immortal jellyfish has the distinction among animals of possibly being able to live forever.   If it becomes sick or old, it can revert to a younger stage of its life. This cycle can repeat over and over.   At least in theory, an immortal jellyfish could live forever, though sometimes these animals are prey to other sea creatures or die of disease.

The scientific species name of the immortal jellyfish is Turritopsis dohrnii.

Loose Goose

The overly fastidious Canadian goose

Fluffed her feathers 'til they all came loose

Being embarrassed at her state of undress

She ordered new feathers to be mailed express

By the Way. . .

Geese are large birds found all over the globe. The word g*eese* is the plural of *goose*. (Nevertheless, *mongooses*, not "mongeese," is the plural of an animal called the *mongoose*. English is sometimes tricky that way.)

Technically, the term *goose* means a female goose. The term g*ander* means a male goose. A famous saying is "What is good for the goose is good for the gander." This means what is good for a man is also good for a woman, or, more generally, what is good for one type of person is also good for another type of person. Here are some other sayings involving geese:

Saying that someone's "goose is cooked" means that they are in trouble.

"Killing the goose that lays the golden eggs" means destroying or rendering useless something that would otherwise bring good fortune. This idiom is from one of Aesop's fables.

"A wild goose chase" is an activity that is a waste of time and effort. (To appreciate this, you might find a real goose, run after it, and try to catch it.)

The most famous goose may be Mother Goose, an imaginary author of fairy tales and nursery rhymes sometimes published as *(Old) Mother Goose's Rhymes*.

There are several species of geese such as the Canada goose and Chinese goose. Geese are waterfowl related to ducks and swans. The scientific name of the group of animals that includes ducks, geese, and swans is Anatidae.

Lord Mouse Detritus

("Detritus" is pronounced di-try'-təs, where 'i' is pronounced like the "i" in "if" and "ə" is pronounced like the "a" in "alone.")

Detritus was a little mouse

With gray fur and bright eyes

He lived inside a dumpster and

Sometimes you'd hear his cries:

"Oh how I hate untidiness

And all this garbage smell!

My fur is stained, my feet are wet,

And I don't eat that well!"

One fateful day a garbage truck

Scooped up his messy home

Then dumped him and the garbage

Toward the gears that grind and groan!

Detritus, though, was nimble, so

He jumped up on the hood

He rode atop without a stop

To where huge mansions stood

"It's ritzy here!" Detritus said.

"It's where I'm meant to be!

I'll bathe and preen and then assume

A new identity!"

He dove into a fountain

He scrubbed himself with leaves

He brushed his teeth with peppermint

Then dried off in the breeze

He spied a statue made of gold

A small hole in its base

"True luxury for me!" he cried

"I've found the perfect place!"

And so, you see, near tragedy

Can lead to something grander

With luck and wits, Detritus sits

As Lord of his small manor

By the Way. . .

About the story: One of the dictionary definitions of "detritus" is: odds and ends.

Mice are small mammals found nearly everywhere on Earth. Because they share many biological attributes with humans, mice are sometimes used by scientists to test new medicines. While it is widely believed that mice like to eat cheese – as often seen in cartoons – in reality mice generally do not like cheese.

Many common expressions involve mice in some way:

"Quiet as a mouse." (This may be said about a person who is quiet or shy.)

"Build a better mousetrap and the world will beat a path to your door." (You will (supposedly) be successful if you invent something that improves on an existing invention.)

"The best laid schemes o' mice an' men Gang aft a-gley [often go awry]." (That line is from *To a Mouse*, a 1786 poem by Robert Burns of Scotland. The title of a novel by American author John Steinbeck, *Of Mice and Men*, is based on that line.)

"When the cat's away the mice will play." (If people are left without someone in authority, they may goof off.)

"Play cat and mouse with someone." (This is about one person (the cat) teasing or chasing another person (the mouse).)

The most famous mouse in the world is probably Mickey Mouse. Mickey first appeared in a 1928 Walt Disney animated film called *Steamboat Willie*. That film has been designated as important to American culture by the U.S. National Film Registry, part of the U.S. Library of Congress.

There are 30 different species of mice with informal names such as house mouse, field mouse, and dormouse. A dormouse attended the Mad Hatter's tea party in *Alice's Adventures in Wonderland* by Lewis Carroll. Mice (and related animals such as hamsters, squirrels, and even beavers) belong to a group of animals that scientists call Rodentia.

Manatee Identity

A manatee

A he or she

Swam in the sea

Calm as can be

But one such she

Said wearily

"I'm not a he.

I'm she, you see.

"I now decree

Equality!

Our name should be

Wo-man-atee!"

By the Way. . .

Manatees are large, plant-eating mammals. Manatees are sometimes called "sea cows" because they are peaceful, slow-moving creatures similar to cows on land. They live in the warm waters of the Caribbean, the Amazon River, and near the west coast of Africa. Manatees must occasionally come to the surface to breathe air, as is true of other mammals that spend most of their time in the sea, such as whales. Manatees maneuver using a pair of flippers and a large, roundish tail. Adults are up to about 13 feet (4 meters) in length and weigh up to about 1,301 pounds (590 kilograms).

Manatees may have something to do with mermaids: mythical creatures that appear to be a woman from the waist up and a fish from the waist down. (Similarly, mermen are half-man / half-fish.) In older times, sailors sometimes reported sighting mermaids. Even Christopher Columbus reported seeing mermaids during his exploration of the Caribbean. These sightings may have been inspired by manatees. But that is just conjecture – perhaps mermaids are real; well, maybe not.

There are three species of manatees. Their scientific names are Trichechus inunguis, Trichechus manatus, and Trichechus senegalensis.

Monster Mystery

The strange Tully Monster lived in the ocean

Three hundred million years ago

They say it swam fast with a wiggling motion

But, alas, we may not ever know

It might have been fierce, it might have been docile

It might have enjoyed eating blueberry pie

But all it is now is a primeval fossil

That helps us to ponder the eons gone by

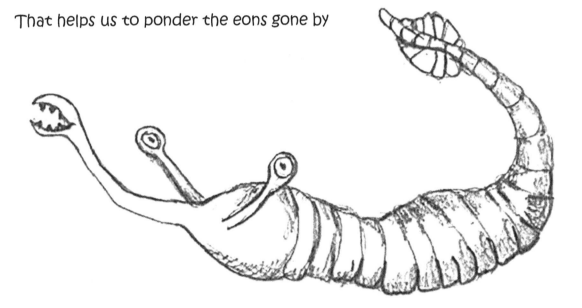

By the Way. . .

In the 1950s, after looking through a coal mine's scrap heap near the city of Chicago in the state of Illinois in the U.S., an amateur fossil collector named Francis Tully discovered a fossil of a previously unknown creature. It has since been informally named the Tully monster, after its discoverer and its rather bizarre appearance.

Only a little is known about the Tully monster. It has been extinct for about 300 million years. It had a primitive backbone and was up to about 14 inches (35 centimeters) long.

It wasn't its size, but the fossil's appearance that earned it the description "monster." (However, keep in mind that, as stated in the title of the original 1956 movie, only Godzilla is actually the "King of the Monsters.") Basically, the Tully Monster had a pair of fins at the back-end of its body, eye-like organs at the end of stalks that stuck out sideways near the upper middle of its body, and a trunk-like snout that stuck out from the front of its body and was tipped with a claw-like mouth with sharp teeth.

The Tully monster's scientific species name is Tullimonstrum gregarium. In the whole world, fossils of this animal have been found only in the state of Illinois. The government of Illinois has named the Tully monster the official state fossil of Illinois.

Moth Ball

A thought occurred to a moth:
I'm tired of eating cloth

So the moth enticed the bee
"Please come to the ball with me

"We'll decorate our wings
And dress like queens and kings

"We'll twirl ourselves around
We'll keep ourselves spellbound

"We'll dance to every tune
We'll dance from May 'til June

"We'll trip the light fantastic
We'll make romantic magic

" 'Neath evening's moonlit sky
We'll dance as time flies by"

By the Way. . .

About the story: "We'll trip the light fantastic" means to dance lightly to music. Similar phrases appear in various books and songs. The phrase is derived from lines in a poem by Englishman John Milton written in 1645: Com, and trip it as ye go, / On the light fantastick toe.

Moths are a type of insect found all over the world. Moths are related to butterflies, though it's not always easy to tell them apart. Butterflies typically have thin antennae with a little bulb at the end, while moths' antennae tend to be feathery in appearance.

Young moths, like young butterflies, are called caterpillars (also known as larvae, the plural of larva). Caterpillars make cocoons from which they emerge as adults with wings. Silk, prized for the smooth cloth that can be made from it, comes from moth cocoons. The best-known moth caterpillar that creates silk is called the silkworm.

Silk aside, moths are often considered to be pests that make life more difficult for humans. Some moths eat crops and some damage trees. Several kinds of moth caterpillars eat fabric such as clothes and blankets made from natural fibers such as wool. Moth balls are man-made items that contain chemicals with a scent that helps repel moths, so people sometimes place moth balls in closets to help protect their clothes.

Some moths have strange, informally assigned names. Examples include the Atlas moth and White Witch moth (both of which have long wingspans), the Madagascan sunset moth (prized by collectors for its beauty), the Death's-head hawkmoth (which can make a squeaking noise), the Bogong moth (a food source for some, apparently very hungry, native Australians), and the Gypsy moth (a pest of some types of trees in North America).

There are estimated to be about 160,000 species of moths, far more than the roughly 18,500 species of butterflies. Moths and butterflies are both in a group of similar animals that scientists have named Lepidoptera. (A person who studies moths and butterflies is called a lepidopterist.)

Naked Mole-Rat

The naked mole-rat went to the seamstress

To try on his first suit of clothes

In the mirror his reflection

Filled him with dejection

Although he had struck his best pose

"Oh, dear, this won't do. You must start anew."

He said to the seamstress and frowned

"I need something chic

To enhance my physique

And look debonair underground!"

The seamstress did sigh

Looked mole in the eye

And said "Sir, I find you quite strange.

You're meant to be nude

And though it sounds rude

Your self-image is what needs to change."

By the Way. . .

Naked mole-rat is the actual name of this small mammal. It grows up to only about 4 inches (10 centimeters) long. It is also sometimes called the sand puppy or the desert mole rat. Like the more familiar mouse and rat, the naked mole-rat is a member of the rodent family.

Naked mole-rats inhabit parts of Africa where they live underground in tunnel systems they build that can be up to about 3 miles (5 kilometers) in length. Naked mole-rats have very little hair covering their wrinkled yellowish or pinkish skin. (Living underground in the darkness probably means appearance is not so important among naked mole-rats.) An unusual trait is that the skin of naked mole-rats does not feel pain.

The mole rat's species name is Heterocephalus glaber. (In case any naked mole-rats happen to be reading this, they should blame scientists for assigning that name.) Although there may not be individual well-known naked mole-rats, this animal species does have some claims to fame. It is the longest living rodent of its size, with lifespans up to about 30 years. And, the journal Science named the naked mole-rat "Vertebrate of the Year" for 2013 due to its natural immunity to certain diseases.

Nervous Tick

 tick in the woods

Was so full of fear

He hadn't the courage

To suck blood from a deer

He grew very hungry

He needed advice

He went to a guru

He'd pay any price

"Dear child," said the guru

"Don't take medication.

To know relaxation

Take up meditation

"Your nerves will calm down

Your mind will be clear

Then feeling no fear

You'll feed from that deer

"You'll have a fine meal

As nature intended

But don't be surprised

if the deer is offended."

By the Way. . .

Ticks are very small, brownish animals. Ticks can be found all over the world but mainly in warm, humid climates.

You may not like to know this if you are squeamish, but ticks feed on the blood of animals, including humans. Ticks cannot jump or fly but may cling to leaves and grasses. They use their legs to grab onto a passing source of blood (such as a hiker). They then bite the animal's skin and secrete a chemical that keeps the blood from clotting. (To be fair, ticks do have at least one redeeming quality: They are sometimes a source of food for birds.)

A type of tick called the deer tick is found in the eastern U.S. and feeds on white-tailed deer. An adult deer tick may be about .1 inch (3 millimeters) long, but longer after feeding on blood.

While ticks may seem like small, annoying insects, they are actually small, annoying arachnids that are a different biological class than insects. Arachnids, the animals in the biological class Arachnida, are 8-legged animals such as mites, scorpions, and spiders, as well as ticks.

Pangolin Pungency

("Pangolin" is pronounced pang'-go-lin, rhyming with "violin.")

Something's running in the brush
On its hind legs, in a rush

Slurping termites, slurping ants
Even slurping grubs perchance

At first glance it looks quite queer
Is it something you should fear?

Should you stay or should you flee?
Oh, whatever could it be?

As it slinks into your view
You will quickly have a clue

Judging from its scaly skin
It must be a pangolin

Since it looks so cute and nice
You will want to pet it twice

Yet, a warning to the wise:
You might get quite a surprise

If it gets annoyed with you
It will spray you with its goo

From its hind end you'll receive
Stench so stinky you will grieve

'Cause their odor can appall
Pangos have no friends at all

Each lives alone in its lair
Playing games of solitaire

By the Way. . .

Pangolins are relatively small mammals that inhabit Africa and Asia. (In this case, "relatively small" means bigger than mice but smaller than deer.) The largest pangolins can be up to 39 inches (100 centimeters) long.

Some pangolins live in underground burrows and others live in hollow trees. Their diet is mainly ants and termites that they capture using their long, thin tongues. Large pangolins can extend their tongues as far as 16 inches (40 centimeters). Pangolins generally live alone and get together only to mate.

Unlike other mammals, pangolin skin is covered with large, hard brown scales for protection. These scales are made of keratin which is also the material in human fingernails. Pangolins can roll up into a ball-like shape in which they are protected by their scales. In fact, the name "pangolin" comes from the Malay word "pengguling" that means "something that rolls up."

Another important way pangolins protect themselves from predators is their ability to emit a noxious odor from glands in their hind end. Pangolins are considered to be among the world's worst smelling animals.

There are eight living species of pangolins. All of them belong to the biological family Manidae.

Perfumed Piglet

little piglet chanced upon

Perfume in an amphora

"It smells divine," exclaimed the swine.

"I adore the flora aura!"

By the Way. . .

<u>About the story</u>: An amphora is a type of pottery that can be used to store liquids. It has a roundish body wider than its neck and sometimes has two handles on opposite sides. Amphoras were common in ancient Greece and Rome.

A piglet is a young domestic pig. Domestic pigs are mammals also known as hogs and swine.   Domestic pigs generally have hairless, pinkish skin. (A few other mammals, such as the rhinoceros and the elephant, also have little to no hair.) A full-grown adult pig can weigh over 700 pounds (318 kilograms). Today, domestic pigs can be found all over the world.

Domestic pigs are intelligent and can be trained to perform simple tasks and tricks. They also have some interesting physical traits. For one, because they have few or no sweat glands, pigs like to wallow in mud to protect themselves from the heat. A particularly unusual trait is that pigs have built-in protection against snake venom.

Fictional pigs have played significant roles in entertainment. Miss Piggy is a famous Muppet. The *Three Little Pigs* is a well-known children's story. A pig that happens to be named Piglet is a character in the *Winnie-the-Pooh* books by A. A. Milne. In *Animal Farm* by George Orwell, a pig named Napoleon becomes a dictator over other animals.

The domesticated pig's species name is Sus domesticus. It is estimated that there are about 1 billion domesticated pigs alive on Earth, making pigs one of the most numerous, relatively large mammals on the planet.

Puppy and Kitten

A puppy named Dickens fell in love with a kitten

Quite smitten was Dickens with Mittens the kitten

But Mittens just wanted to play like a cat

With yarn balls and toy mice and fun things like that

Dickens tried to amuse her with all his best tricks

He jumped and rolled over and fetched her some sticks

But Mittens just blinked and was never impressed

She decided that Dickens was simply a pest

Love can be lovely when both souls are smitten

But love can be hard between puppy and kitten

By the Way. . .

It is estimated that there are over 500 million cats in the world, and even more dogs. They can be found all over the globe. Virtually everyone is familiar with these animals and we've already had a lot to say about cats in *Kitty Go Lightly*, so we'll just say a few words here about kittens and puppies.

"Kitty" or "kitten" means a young cat. "Kitty" is also a name given to some human females or may be a nickname for full names such as Kathryn. The domestic cat's scientific species name is Felis catus which is related to the word "feline."

"Puppy" or "pup" means a young dog. The scientific species name for dog is Canis lupus familiaris. Fans of the *Harry Potter* stories by J. K. Rowling may notice that Professor Lupin's name is similar to "lupus." That is likely not a coincidence because the professor is a werewolf and wolves are closely related to dogs.

There are many breeds of domestic cats, such as Abyssinian, American shorthair, Burmese, Persian, and Siamese. There are many breeds of dogs, such as boxers, golden retrievers, poodles, Yorkshire Terriers, and beagles. (A famous beagle is Snoopy, a character in the Peanuts comic strip and animated films.)

Relevant Elephant

A cruel man hunting for ivory once said

"Who cares about elephants, anyway?"

When heard by a herd, the elephants said

"Please listen, we've something to say!

"Our ivory is part of our essence, you see

To us, our long tusks are quite dear

We just want to roam and be happy and free

Your callousness fills us with fear"

"I beg your forgiveness," the hunter implored

"Your passion makes me realize

Your right to live freely should not be ignored

A truth I now see with new eyes"

By the Way. . .

<u>About the story</u>: Sadly, elephants are an endangered species due to poachers killing them to retrieve and sell their ivory tusks. That's because ivory has sometimes been used to make piano keys, works of art, and more. (Today, other materials can be used.) To help preserve elephants, many countries, including the U.S., have limited the sale of ivory.

Elephants are very large, grayish, plant-eating mammals that live in parts of Africa and Asia. They are notable for their long trunks, large ears, and ivory tusks. Male African elephants, the largest living land animals, can weigh up to about 15,000 pounds (7,000 kilograms) and live up to 70 years in the wild.

Humans have used elephants for centuries for tasks such as hauling goods and riding. Historically, elephants were sometimes used to help fight wars because they are strong and because their size can intimidate enemies. In Thailand, elephants are used to digest coffee beans for making a brand of coffee called Black Ivory coffee. (The elephants eat the beans, their digestive systems break down the beans' proteins that contribute to coffee's bitterness, and the excreted beans are harvested. That image may not be very appetizing to coffee drinkers.)

Elephants have long played important roles in human culture. For example, an important Hindu deity, the elephant-headed Ganesha, is associated with writers and is believed to be able to grant people's desires. In Islamic tradition, the year when Muhammad was born, 570, is known as the Year of the Elephant.

The Indian fable about the *blind men and an elephant* is about a group of blind persons that each touch a different part of an elephant (such as the trunk, a side, and the tail), leading each person to think the elephant has a very different appearance. The lesson is that a partial view of something may not reveal everything about it.

There are three species of elephants: the African bush elephant, the African forest elephant, and the Asian elephant. These species all belong to a group of animals that scientists call Elephantidae. Mammoths, now extinct, also belong to that group.

Seal of Approval

A young seal once pondered a subjective question:

Do I like my seal-ness, upon self-reflection?

I don't want this quest to become an obsession

I'll just strive for honest and fair introspection

The downside has things mother nature left out

I'm lacking a whale's magnificent spout

I envy a seagull's most marvelous wings

And jellyfish with their long menacing stings

The upside has wonderful things I can do

I can move over land and in the sea, too

My eyes see quite well in both water and air

And I really like the smooth fur that I wear

No one can have every possible trait

To be just one species is everyone's fate

I think I've discovered how I really feel

I truly take pride in my life as a seal

By the Way. . .

Seals are mammals that are highly adapted to living on land and swimming in the water. Most are found in the cold waters of both the northern and southern hemispheres. While they move a bit awkwardly on land, seals can swim gracefully through water because their limbs are flippers. Different species of seals range significantly in size. The Baikal seal is just a few feet (one meter or so) in length while some seals, called southern elephant seals, grow up to about 19 feet (5.8 meters) in length.

Seals have played various roles in human culture for a long time. Irish and Scottish folklore speaks of the silkie (also spelled *selkie),* seals that could change into human form and walk on land. An ancient Greek coin depicts the head of a seal; the Greeks believed that seals loved both the sea and sun and were considered to be under the protection of the gods Poseidon and Apollo. Seals are relatively intelligent and playful animals, and have sometimes been trained to perform tricks.

There are 33 living species of seals. All seals belong to a group of animals that scientists call Pinnipedia. All members of that group are informally called seals, including walruses and sea lions.

Smug Slug

The blue angel slug casts a feathery shade

As it floats silver blue on the sea

Admiring its reflection

Of sunlit perfection

It thinks "What a beautiful me!"

But this beauty hides an unpleasant surprise:

Feathered "fingers" that sting painfully

It's not that it's mean,

It's its nature you see,

So don't touch this slug hastily!

95

By the Way. . .

The blue angel slug is a type of mollusk, like clams and oysters but without a shell. It lives in tropical waters. Blue angel slugs have a striking, eerily beautiful appearance, and do not look anything like land-based slugs that are more worm-like.

These creatures grow up to only about 1.2 inches (3 centimeters) long. They float upside down on the water and are carried along by winds and ocean currents.

Blue angel slugs have two main protections against predators. First, their coloring provides camouflage. The side of the slug that faces up is blue which blends with the blue of the water if seen from above. The side that faces down is silver/grey which blends with the surface of the water if seen from below. Second, this slug has what looks like feather-like "fingers" around parts of its body. Any animal, including humans, touching these fingers will feel a painful sting. A word to the wise: If you ever happen to see a blue angel slug washed ashore, look but don't touch.

The scientific species name of the blue angel slug is Glaucus atlanticus. Informal names for this animal are blue angel, blue dragon, blue glaucus, blue ocean slug, blue sea slug, and sea swallow.

Snake Spits

The spitting cobra

Was a terrible guest

He spat on the rug and the floor.

"I'd invite him again,"

Said the python, his friend,

"But I'd give him a big cuspidor!"

By the Way. . .

About the poem: "Cuspidor" is a rather old term for something also called a "spittoon." Cuspidors are vase-like receptacles that men (perhaps only men) who chewed tobacco used to spit into.

Snakes are reptiles that have long bodies without legs. They move by using their muscles and scales to help propel them forward. A cobra is one kind of snake. Most cobras are venomous and are easily recognized because they are able to rear up and display a hood that frames their head area.

A spitting cobra is a particular type of cobra found in Africa and Asia. In addition to being able to bite, spitting cobras can squirt venom from their fangs as a form of self-defense. The venom can be projected up to over 6 feet (about 2 meters) away. Although that venom is harmless if on only the surface of a person's skin, it could cause severe pain and even blindness if in contact with an eye. Spitting cobras have apparently figured this out because they actually aim for the eyes.

In some Asian and Middle Eastern countries, such as India and Egypt, persons known as snake charmers entertain audiences by pretending to hypnotize cobras that rise out of a basket. The charmer may play a pipe implying the cobra is dancing to the music, but cobras are more likely just following the swaying movement of the snake charmer and pipe. Snake charming goes back centuries, but the number of practitioners these days is smaller than in the past.

As if one species of a spitting cobra wouldn't be enough, there are actually several species of just this one type of cobra. All cobras – in fact, all snakes – belong to a group of animals that scientists call Reptilia. In addition to snakes, Reptilia also contains other animals such as crocodiles, lizards, and turtles.

The Swift's Tailor

I'm a bird called a swift

But I couldn't fly fast

The other swifts teased me

As they soared on past

They mocked me and said

"In fleetness you fail

You're slow as a sloth

You're slow as a snail."

I felt out of place

I started to panic

I needed some help

To be aerodynamic

A tailorbird eyed me

From hind end to beak

"I'll make something for you

Come back in a week."

99

I returned as he asked

He said "Give this a try.

Wearing this, Mr. Swift,

You will fly fast and high.

"It's a Superman cape

I made just for you.

As fast as an arrow

You'll soar through the blue!"

So now I can soar

Over valleys and cliffs

And I am the swiftest

Of all of the swifts!

By the Way. . .

About swifts

Swifts are a type of bird that can be found on every continent except Antarctica. Their feathers are generally black or brown. The smallest kinds of swifts are about 3.5 inches (9 centimeters) long while the largest kinds of swifts are up to about 10 inches (25 centimeters) long.

Some kinds of swifts have the fastest flying speed of any bird. The speed of one kind of swift, called the common swift, has been measured as fast as 70 miles (113 kilometers) per hour.

There are about 100 species of swifts, all in a group of animals that scientists call Apodidae. That group name is derived from a Greek term that means "footless" because swifts have tiny, weak feet and cannot perch, though they can cling to vertical surfaces such as cliffs.

About tailorbirds

Tailorbirds are small birds found in tropical areas of Asia. Their upper bodies are green while their lower bodies are a creamy color. In *The Jungle Book* by Rudyard Kipling, the story *Rikki-Tikki-Tavi* includes a tailorbird couple.

Tailorbirds get their name from the way they build their nests. They pierce the edges of a large leaf and sew the edges together with plant fibers or spider's web to make a cup-like container in which they build a grass nest.

There are multiple species of tailorbirds with informal names such as common tailorbird, dark-necked tailorbird, and black-headed tailorbird. Most tailorbirds belong to a group of birds that scientists call Orthotomus.

Teeth of the Tiger

The tiger's teeth are razor sharp

He likes his meat with sauce

After he dines he grabs some vines

To use as dental floss

By the Way. . .

Tigers are mammals and are the largest types of cats. They are even larger than the other large cats they are related to including jaguars, leopards, and lions. Today, tigers live in parts of Asia from as far south as India to as far north as Siberia.

A tiger's fur has dark vertical stripes. For most tigers, the fur between the stripes is mostly reddish-orange on the sides and upper part of their bodies, and whitish near the underside of their bodies and parts of their heads. Some tigers, appropriately called white tigers, have all white fur between their stripes and enchanting blue eyes.

Tigers have long influenced human culture. Here are a few examples. Tigers are the national animal of Bangladesh, India, Malaysia, and South Korea. In *The Jungle Book* by Rudyard Kipling, the tiger Shere Khan is the enemy of the boy Mowgli. In *Life of Pi* by Yann Martel, the story of a young man who ends up sharing a small boat with a tiger, the part of the story where the tiger swims is based on the fact that tigers really are good swimmers. Calling something "a paper tiger" means it seems powerful but actually is not. *The Tyger*, a famous poem by the English author William Blake published in 1794, begins

> Tyger! Tyger! burning bright,
>
> In the forests of the night

Scientists consider all types of tigers to be a single species called Panthera tigris. However, scientists also define several subspecies such as Malayan tigers and Bengal tigers. White tigers are a rare type of Bengal tiger.

Unhuggable Puggle

("Echidna" is pronounced i-kid'-nah, where "i" is pronounced as the "i" in "if.")

Echidnas are rare and live in Australia

Or sometimes New Guinea with other Mammalia

As newborns, they're hairless, and shiny, and wet

They're sometimes called puggles, a coveted pet

But once they grow up to bowling ball size

They're spikey and spiny, right up to their eyes!

Now, how can you pet a pet that's so prickly?

Ever so lightly and ever so quickly!

By the Way. . .

Echidnas are small, spiny mammals that inhabit Australia and New Guinea. They were named after Echidna, a creature from Greek mythology that was half-woman and half-snake, because echidnas were thought to have characteristics of both mammals and reptiles. Perhaps the Greeks noticed that echidnas are among the very few kinds of mammals that lay eggs, in contrast to birds and most reptiles.

Echidnas are very timid. If they sense danger, they try to bury themselves or to curl into a ball. Their spines then help protect them from predators.

The echidna diet consists mainly of ants and termites (which may make readers glad they are not echidnas). Echidnas are sometimes called spiny anteaters. However, echidnas are not closely related to the anteaters of the Americas. Although echidnas' young are called puggles, they should not be confused with the breed of dogs that have that same name.

Echidnas have influenced human culture. An echidna is shown on one side of the Australian five-cent coin. One of the mascots of the 2000 Summer Olympics was an echidna named Millie, a name referring to the year 2000 marking a new *mill*ennium. And, Knuckles the Echidna is featured in the video game series Sonic the Hedgehog, though it would take a powerful imagination to tell that Knuckles looks anything like a real echidna.

There are several specifies of echidnas. Echidnas, along with platypuses, belong to a group of animals that scientists call Monotremata. The members of that group are the only living mammals that lay eggs.

Wannabe Wallaby

Living deep in Australia's interior

Suffering a complex quite inferior

Lacking a kangaroo's pedigree

A wallaby suffers anxiety

"I'm too short to hop over boulders," says she,

"And lack a roo's boxing agility.

But I've got a pouch; I'm sure that will do

To hold all my joeys, like a true kangaroo!"

By the Way. . .

<u>About the story</u>: "A complex inferior" refers to something usually called an "inferiority complex," a term describing someone who lacks self-confidence. A "pedigree" is a history of a person's or an animal's ancestors. A "joey" is a very young wallaby or kangaroo.

Wallabies are small to medium size mammals with brownish or grayish fur. They are closely related to kangaroos and, in fact, look like small kangaroos. (From a wallaby's perspective, however, it may be preferable to say that kangaroos look like big wallabies.) Both wallabies and kangaroos are plant eaters. Like young kangaroos, young wallabies are called joeys; a joey spends much of its early life in its mother's pouch. Also, like kangaroos, wallabies have short forelegs and larger, powerful hind legs. A predator or anyone else a wallaby or kangaroo doesn't like that gets too close may find itself on the receiving end of a strong kick.

Wallabies were originally found only in Australia and on the nearby island of New Guinea. Australia's affection for these animals is reflected in a popular rugby team named the Wallabies. Some wallabies have been brought to other countries by humans. For example, there are a few wild wallabies in England whose ancestors escaped from a zoo.

There are several different species of wallabies. They have informal names such as the red-necked wallaby and the rock-wallaby. All wallaby species belong to a group of animals that scientists call Marsupialia. Marsupials are mammals that carry their young in a pouch. In addition to wallabies, examples of marsupials are kangaroos, koalas, possums, and Tasmanian devils.

Warthog's Wallow

The warthog loves to wallow in mud

And practice introspection

"It's such a tonic, this squishy goo,

So good for my complexion!"

By the Way. . .

Warthogs are dark-colored, medium-sized mammals found in parts of Africa. Warthogs are related to domestic pigs. However, these two types of animals have some significant differences. In particular, warthogs have four sharp tusks, giving warthogs a fierce appearance.

Also, unlike domestic pigs, warthogs' heads are covered with bumps. Although the similar appearance of these bumps to skin warts led to the animal's name, these bumps are a normal part of a warthog's body. (Actual warts on the skin are small growths that are a type of infection.)

Warthogs like to wallow in mud to cool down and to avoid irritating insects such as ticks. Oddly, tickbirds, such as the oxpecker, sometimes sit on a warthog and eat ticks found on the warthog's skin. (If the reader has heard of the oxpecker before, congratulations!)

There are two species of warthogs. The most widespread species is informally called the common warthog (or, simply, warthog) and has the scientific species name Phacochoerus africanus. The less widespread species is informally called the desert warthog and has the scientific species name Phacochoerus aethiopicus.

A video side-trip: To see a video showing a warthog quietly resting in the mud while being "cleaned" by oxpeckers, search https://www.youtube.com for warthog oxpecker.

Weevil Upheaval

A little boll weevil was sleeping one night

In his soft silky cotton ball bed

Then all of a sudden he woke with a start

When a booming noise rattled his head

"Good grief," cried the weevil. "What sound is so evil

To waken me with such a scare?"

He looked all about, down his long pointy snout

In fear that a monster was there

But to his surprise he only laid eyes

On a firefly twinkling its light

"You saw it?" asked weevil. The firefly laughed.

"Yes, 'cause it's still in plain sight."

"But where?" said the weevil "I see nothing here,

My head hurts, I'm feeling quite rotten."

Said the firefly "Please! 'Twas your thunderous sneeze.

Perhaps you're allergic to cotton."

By the Way. . .

The boll weevil is a type of insect called a beetle. Beetles (not to be confused with what the authors consider to be the best band ever!) have thin shell-like protections over parts of their bodies. The adult boll weevil is quite small, usually less than about ¼-inch (6 millimeters) long. It is blackish, brownish, or grayish in color and has a long snout.

The boll weevil feeds primarily on the buds and flowers of cotton plants. The boll weevil originated in the warm, cotton-growing climate of Mexico. From there it spread to cotton-growing areas of the lower United States and South America.

The boll weevil can cause considerable damage to cotton crops. To deal with the situation, some cotton farmers replaced cotton crops with peanut crops. In addition, many regions have programs in place to try to eradicate the boll weevil altogether.

The boll weevil has the scientific species name Anthonomus grandis. (It should be mentioned that it is unlikely boll weevils can actually sneeze.)

A video side trip: To see videos of various singers singing an American folk song about a conversation between a farmer and a boll weevil that is "looking for a home," search https://www.youtube.com for *boll weevil song*.

Wistful Worm

A wistful worm once cleared its throat
And then these words were spoken
"Like all earthworms I have 5 hearts
But each of them is broken.

"I have no friends, I'm all alone
All folks treat me with scorn
They say that I am truly vile
And should not have been born.

"But wait! My luck's about to change
I've found a four leaf clover
With luck I'll start my life anew
My old life will be over.

"Perhaps a death worm I'll become
The kind that makes folks cower
They'll bow before my fearsome size
They'll all be in my power.

"But wishful thinking by itself

Alone can't change my story

It's up to me to change my life

Not merely wish for glory."

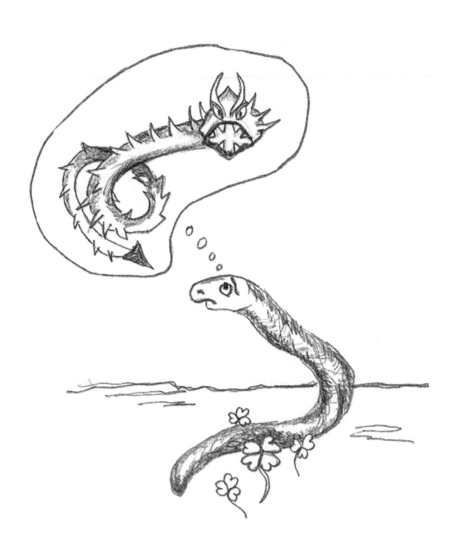

By the Way. . .

<u>About the story</u>: The Mongolian death worm is an intimidating, mythological creature several feet long that exists in the Gobi Desert of Mongolia. It can supposedly kill at a distance and is so poisonous that just touching it results in instant death.

Worms are animals that have tube-shaped bodies and no arms or legs. Worms can be found nearly everywhere on earth.

Although some people may think that all worms are the same, there are actually many different kinds of worms. One difference that is easy to see is size. The smallest worms are microscopic in size. In contrast, the largest type of worm, the bootlace worm, is up to about 180 feet (55 meters) long and about 3.9 inches (10 centimeters) wide. (In case their size isn't impressive enough, bootlace worms also have poisonous mucus. It would probably not make a good pet.)

Some worms are parasites that can live in another animal's body with unpleasant consequences. For example, people who eat uncooked meat may be infected by tapeworms that take up residence in the intestine. (Ugh!) Cats and dogs are sometimes infected by worms such as roundworms that also live in the intestine.

In spite of mythical death worms and actual worm parasites, it must be mentioned that some worms do good things. Earthworms, in particular,]increase the amount of water and air that gets into soil, helping plants in gardens and farms grow better.

There are thousands of different species of worms. Scientists estimate there are about three thousand different species of earthworms alone. Some informal names for different species of worms are earthworms, flatworms, inchworms, ribbon worms, roundworms, tapeworms, and velvet worms.

<u>A video side trip</u>: To see videos about the Mongolian death worm, search https://www.youtube.com for *Mongolian death worm.*

Vain Crane

crane was flying over Spain

When it flew into pouring rain

Which soaked it through, to its disdain

Because it was so very vain

It landed on the nearest plain

Where it could hide 'til dry again

By the Way. . .

About the story: The title *Crane in Spain* is based on the saying "The rain in Spain stays mainly in the plain." This phrase became famous as a song in the Broadway musical *My Fair Lady* which was based on the play *Pygmalion* by George Bernard Shaw. Perfectionists have pointed out that rain in Spain actually falls mainly in the northern mountains.

Cranes are relatively large birds with long legs and long necks. Cranes live on every continent except Antarctica and South America. They eat some kinds of plants and some small animals such as fish and insects.

Cranes are beautiful birds that have been used symbolically in many cultures worldwide. For example, in Japan the crane symbolizes good fortune and long life. The crane is a popular subject of the Japanese art of origami (paper folding). An ancient Japanese legend is that a crane will grant a wish to anyone who folds a thousand origami cranes.

There are multiple species of cranes in a group of animals that scientists call Gruidae. Informal names for some of these species are whooping crane (named for its loud calls) and snow crane (named for its nearly all-white color).

Farewell – An Aye-Aye Bye

Adios
Spanish

さようなら
Japanese

Goodbye
English

הֱיֵה שׁלום
Hebrew

Aloha
Hawaiian

Auf Wiedersehen
German

وداعا
Arabic

Arrivederci
Italian

Au Revoir
French

Uh, oh, how did this happen?

I see you've found me again

We can't go on meeting this way

Like all ~~tails~~ tales, this must end

(How clever of me - I made a pun!)

It's Time to End

Where to Find More Information About the Animals

Much more information is known about each animal than could be included in the short "By the Way" discussions. Readers are encouraged to look up more information about animals they find especially interesting. A good source of information is the World Wide Web. Just two of many useful general-purpose websites are https://www.wikipedia.org for details and images, and https://www.youtube.com for videos.

The following list identifies some of the organizations that promote and provide information about animal conservation:

- International Union for Conservation of Nature (IUCN), https://www.iucn.org/. IUCN publishes a "red list" of the conservation status of individual species at http://www.iucnredlist.org/.

- World Wildlife Fund (WWF), https://www.worldwildlife.org/. WWF publishes a list of the conservation status of individual species at https://www.worldwildlife.org /species/directory.

- Zoological Society of London (ZSL), https://www.zsl.org/. ZSL's website states: "ZSL runs conservation programmes in Britain and over 50 countries worldwide; the conservation of wild animals and their natural habitats is fundamental to our mission."

World Map

This map can help readers find most of the geographical areas mentioned in this book. A map like this that projects the globe onto a flat surface is called a Mercator map. The locations and shapes of areas are approximations. The names of cities are each preceded by a dot to more precisely indicate their location. The areas of North America, Europe, and Asia are in larger, light gray letters. Only some country borders are shown.

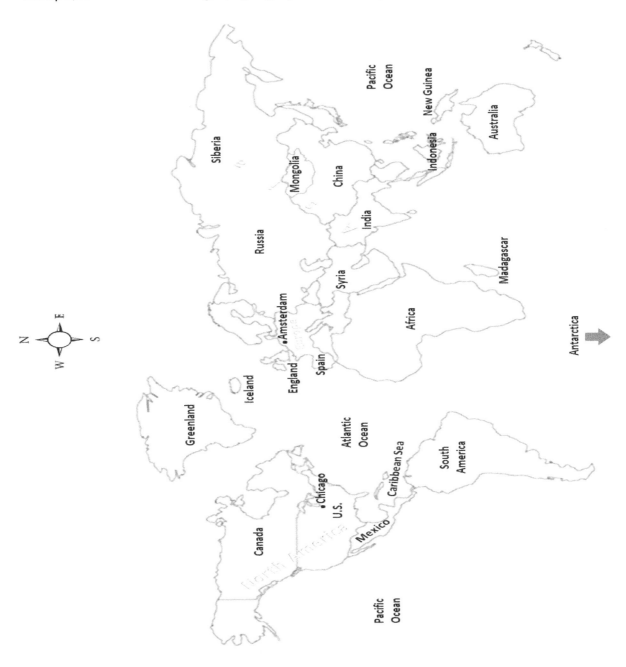

About the Authors and Illustrator

Robin Strand is both co-author and illustrator of Critterlandia. Robin originated the concept of Critterlandia and easily persuaded David to join her in creating this book. She also paints and creates whimsical pottery. Beyond this book, Robin further expresses her love of animals by volunteering at a local zoo and by attending adoringly to her two cats, Seamus and Vincent.

David Sacks is co-author of Critterlandia. David previously worked in the computer industry and published two books on computer technology. After retiring from the world of computers, he embarked on a very different adventure in working with Robin on Critterlandia, contributing to the poetry and also writing the By the Way discussions.